For Geraldine, Joe, Naomi,
Eddie, Laura, and Isaac
M.R.

For Amelia
H.O.

First published 1989 by
Walker Books Ltd, 87 Vauxhall Walk
London SE11 5HJ

This edition published 2001

10 9 8 7 6

Text © 1989 Michael Rosen
Illustrations © 1989 Helen Oxenbury

Printed in Singapore

British Library Cataloguing in Publication Data:
a catalogue record for this book is
available from the British Library.

ISBN 0-7445-8190-7

www.walkerbooks.co.uk

We're Going on a Bear Hunt

Retold by
Michael Rosen

Illustrated by
Helen Oxenbury

WALKER BOOKS
AND SUBSIDIARIES
LONDON · BOSTON · SYDNEY · AUCKLAND

We're going on a bear hunt.

We're going to catch a big one.

What a beautiful day!

We're not scared.

Uh-uh! Grass!
Long wavy grass.
We can't go over it.
We can't go under it.

Oh no!
We've got to go through it!

Swishy swashy!
Swishy swashy!
Swishy swashy!

We're going on a bear hunt.

We're going to catch a big one.

What a beautiful day!

We're not scared.

Uh-uh! A river!
A deep cold river.
We can't go over it.
We can't go under it.

Oh no!
We've got to go through it!

Splash splosh!
Splash splosh!
Splash splosh!

We're going on a bear hunt.

We're going to catch a big one.

What a beautiful day!

We're not scared.

Uh-uh! Mud!

Thick oozy mud.

We can't go over it.

We can't go under it.

Oh no!

We've got to go through it!

Squelch squerch!
Squelch squerch!
Squelch squerch!

We're going on a bear hunt.
We're going to catch a big one.
What a beautiful day!
We're not scared.

Uh-uh! A forest!

A big dark forest.

We can't go over it.

We can't go under it.

Oh no!

We've got to go through it!

Stumble trip!
Stumble trip!
Stumble trip!

a bear hunt again.

Uh-uh! A cave!
A narrow gloomy cave.
We can't go over it.
We can't go under it.

Oh no!
We've got to go through it!

We're going on a bear hunt.

We're going to catch a big one.

What a beautiful day!

We're not scared.

We're going on a bear hunt.

We're going to catch a big one.

What a beautiful day!

We're not scared.

We're not going on

Shut the door.

Back upstairs.

Into the bedroom.

Into bed.

Under the covers.

Get to our front door.

Open the door.

Up the stairs.

Oh no!

We forgot to shut the door.

Back downstairs.

Back through the mud! Squelch squerch! Squelch squerch!

Back through the river! Splash splosh! Splash splosh! Splash splosh!

Back through the grass! Swishy swashy! Swishy swashy!

Quick! Back through the cave! Tiptoe! Tiptoe! Tiptoe!

Back through the snowstorm! Hoooo wooooo! Hoooo wooooo!

Back through the forest! Stumble trip! Stumble trip! Stumble trip!

Hoooo woooo!
Hoooo woooo!
Hoooo woooo!

Uh-uh! A snowstorm!

A swirling whirling snowstorm.

We can't go over it.

We can't go under it.

Oh no!

We've got to go through it!

One shiny wet nose!

Two big furry ears!

Two big goggly eyes!

IT'S A BEAR!!!!

Tiptoe!
Tiptoe!
Tiptoe!
WHAT'S THAT?